FIRST DAY JITTERS

by Carson Embrey

Copyright © 2023 FIRST DAY JITTERS by Carson Embrey

All rights reserved. No part of this publication may be reproduced, distributed, or transmitted in any form or by any means, including photocopying, recording, or other electronic or mechanical methods, without the prior written permission of the publisher, except in the case of brief quotations embodied in critical reviews and certain other noncommercial uses permitted by copyright law. For permission requests, write to the publisher, addressed "Attention: Permissions Coordinator," at the email address below.

ISBN# 9798394007514

Cover, illustrations, typesetting and formatting by Jon Klassen.

Carson Embrey - carson.embrey@gmail.com

Dedicated to my first group of students

With summer now over, it's scary to say

I've been a little more than nervous for this day.

Endless pool days and vacations galore,
The glitz and the glamor of summer no more.

The first day back is always a bore. There are lots of things to unpack when I walk through the door.

Box after box,
I'm starting to see
the disheveled classroom
where my students will be.

There's a lot to do and no time to waste!

I need to get busy! I need to make haste!

The decorations are up, and the bookshelves are stocked.
Things are coming together. Man, this is a lot!

With things now in order
it's now easier to see

this is a place where my students will want to be!

A place to learn, a place to grow, a place to wonder.

Oh, I can't wait to see all the mysteries we'll uncover!

The time is near that the students will be here.

Excuse my frankness
but I should say

that I'm feeling quite anxious about the day.

What will I say, or what will I do?
What if I accidentally trip over my shoe?

I hope they remember that this will be my first time meeting them too.

What if

THIS?

and what about

THAT?

I don't need to worry and that's a fact!

Without the stink and without the stank,
I'm hoping all the sweating can wait.

How embarrassing would that be
to start the year with a sweaty catastrophe?

I'm being a little crazy.
I'm being really silly.

Everything will be fine... really!

A whole new group is finally here
and it's time for the start of a brand new school year!

You come to the door and it is clear to me
that maybe you're just as nervous as I seem to be.

Put your worry aside, come through the door.

There are so many things that we're going to explore.

$7 + \boxed{?} = 11$

$\boxed{?} + 13 = 24$

$9 + \boxed{?} = 17$

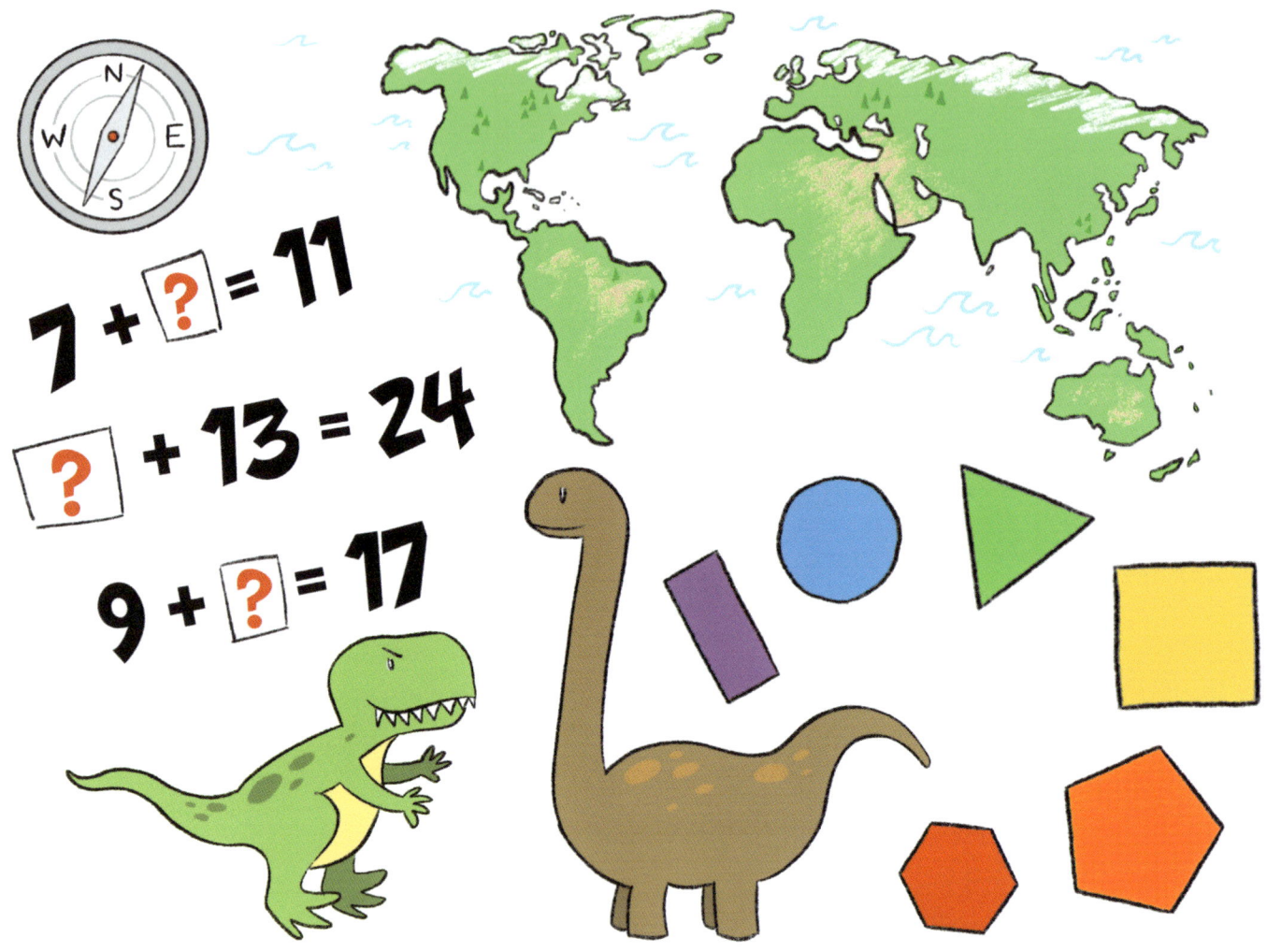

As we enter the room you will see all the new possibilities!

New faces may stare, but don't be scared.
I'm sure you'll have at least one new friend out there.

I'll help you all in, we'll put away our stuff.
Let's give things a chance before we huff and we puff.

Everyone's in and it's time to begin the very first lesson...

so let's all dive in!

I hope it's a success,
I hope you're impressed,

because this may be
the most important three-question test!

It's not for a grade.
Please don't be dismayed,

I just thought it would be a fun game to play.

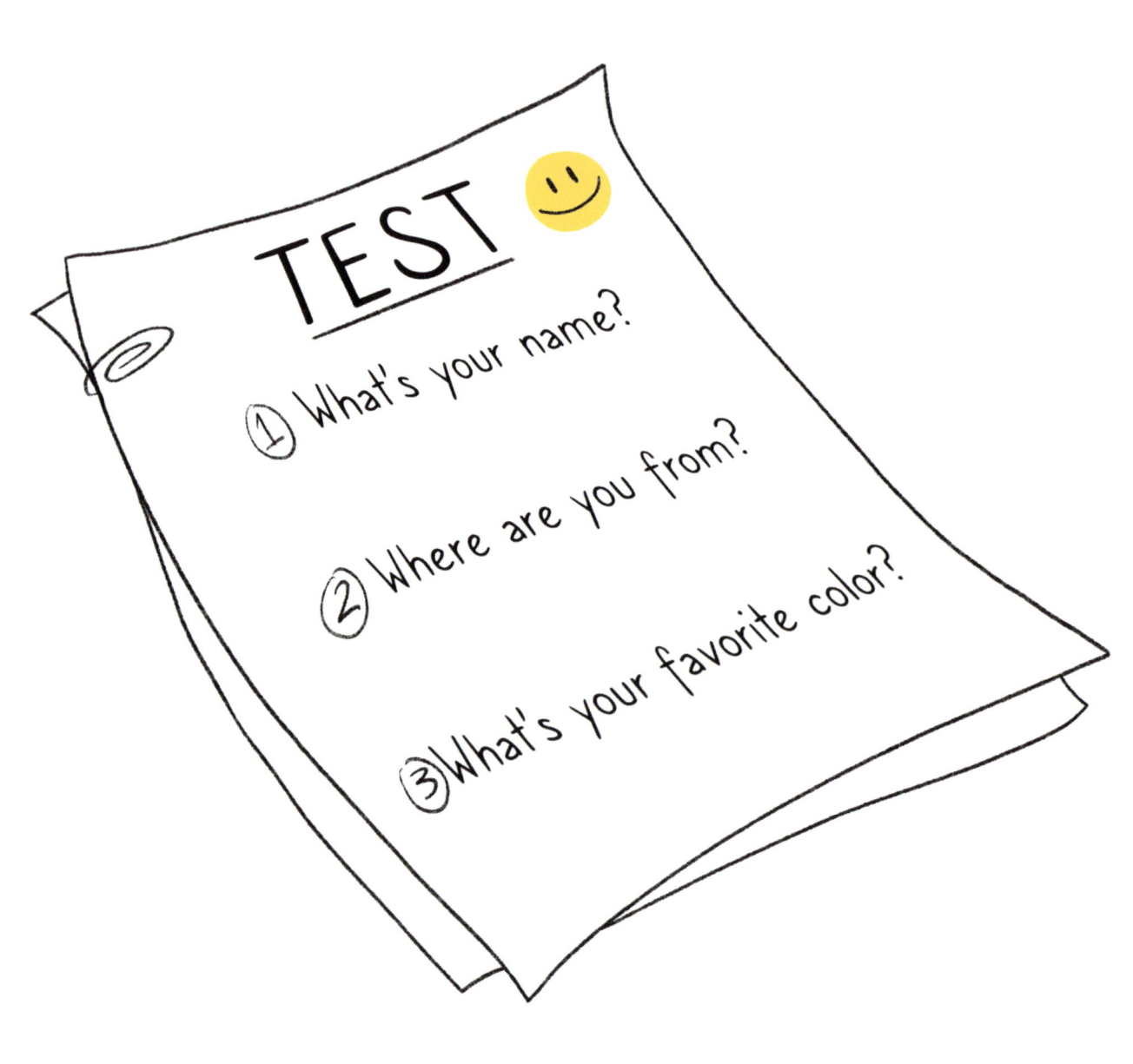

RED? GREEN? YELLOW? PINK?

If you had to guess mine what would you think?

Tik-tok, there goes the clock letting us know it's time to go.

We will pack your things and say goodbye,

followed by a long sorrowful sigh.

After we talked and after we laughed,
we found that our fears had finally passed.

Today was a success
but will be unlike the rest
because the best has yet to come!

HASTE To do something in a hurry or with great speed

FRANKNESS To say something with honesty

ANXIOUS To feel worried about something

CATASTROPHE An event that cause great harm or suffering

DISMAY To feel upset about something

SORROW To feel sad

Printed in Dunstable, United Kingdom

66291996R00022